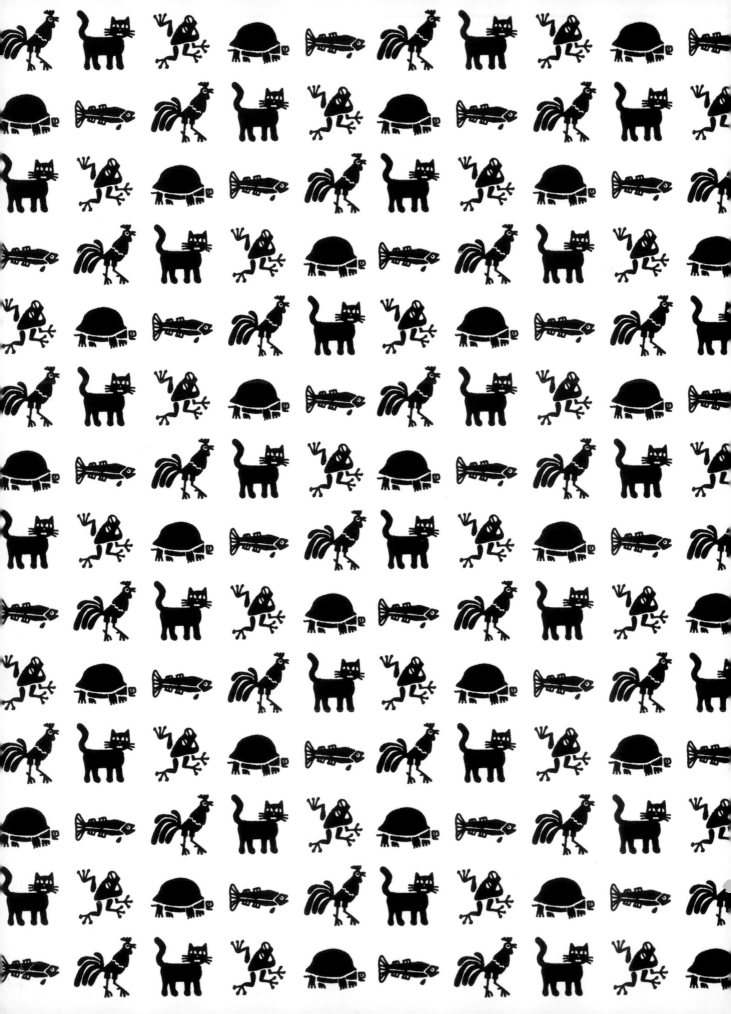

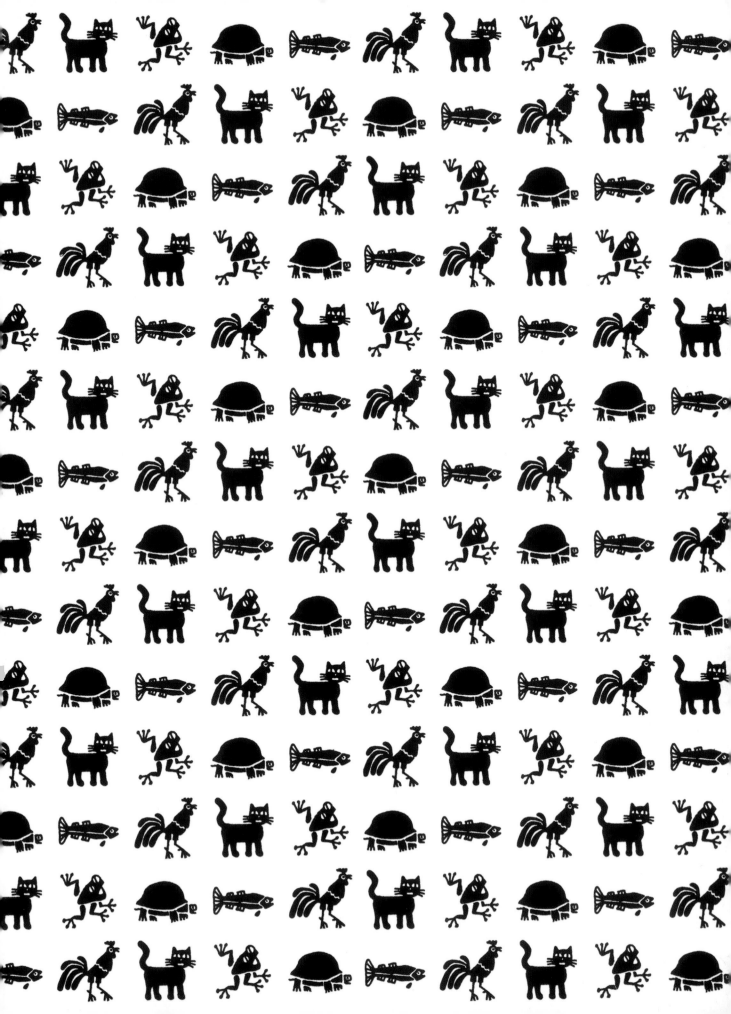

Some other picture books by Eric Carle

1, 2, 3 TO THE ZOO
THE BAD-TEMPERED LADYBIRD
DO YOU WANT TO BE MY FRIEND?
DRAW ME A STAR
LITTLE CLOUD
MISTER SEAHORSE
THE MIXED-UP CHAMELEON
ROOSTER'S OFF TO SEE THE WORLD
"SLOWLY, SLOWLY, SLOWLY," SAID THE SLOTH
THE TINY SEED
TODAY IS MONDAY
THE VERY HUNGRY CATERPILLAR

With Bill Martin Jr

BROWN BEAR, BROWN BEAR, WHAT DO YOU SEE?
PANDA BEAR, PANDA BEAR, WHAT DO YOU SEE?
POLAR BEAR, POLAR BEAR, WHAT DO YOU HEAR?

PUFFIN BOOKS

Published by the Penguin Group
Penguin Books Ltd, 80 Strand, London WC2R 0RL, England
Penguin Group (USA), Inc., 375 Hudson Street, New York, New York 10014, USA
Penguin Books Australia Ltd, 707 Collins Street, Melbourne, Victoria 3008, Australia
Penguin Books Canada Ltd, 10 Alcorn Avenue, Toronto, Ontario, Canada M4V 3B2
Penguin Books India (P) Ltd, 11 Community Centre, Panchsheel Park, New Delhi – 110 017, India
Penguin Group (NZ), cnr Airborne and Rosedale Roads, Albany, Auckland 1310, New Zealand
Penguin Books (South Africa) (Pty) Ltd, Block D, Rosebank Office Park, 181 Jan Smuts Avenue,
Parktown North, Gauteng 2193, South Africa

Penguin Books Ltd, Registered Offices: 80 Strand, London WC2R 0RL, England

puffinbooks.com

First published in Great Britain in this edition by Hamish Hamilton 1995
Published in Puffin Books 1996

021

Copyright © Eric Carle, 1972
All rights reserved

Printed and bound in China

British Library Cataloguing in Publication Data
A CIP catalogue record for this book is available from the British Library

ISBN-13: 978-0-14055-678-0

Rooster's Off to
See the World

ERIC CARLE

PUFFIN BOOKS

One fine morning, a rooster decided that he wanted to travel.
So, right then and there, he set out to see the world.
He hadn't walked very far when he began to feel lonely.

Just then, he met two cats. The rooster said
to them, "Come along with me to see the world."
The cats liked the idea of a trip very much.
"We would love to," they purred and set off down
the road with the rooster.

As they wandered on, the rooster and the
cats met three frogs. "How would you like to
come with us to see the world?" asked the
rooster, eager for more company.
"Why not?" answered the frogs.
"We are not busy now." So the frogs jumped
along behind the rooster and the cats.

After a while, the rooster, the cats, and the frogs saw four turtles crawling slowly down the road.

"Hey," said the rooster, "how would you like to see the world?"

"It might be fun," snapped one of the turtles and they joined the others.

As the rooster, the cats, the frogs, and the turtles walked
along, they came to five fish swimming in the brook.
"Where are you going?" asked the fish.
"We're off to see the world," answered the rooster.
"May we come along?" pleaded the fish.
"Delighted to have you," the rooster replied.
And so the fish came along to see the world.

The sun went down. It began to get dark. The moon came up over the horizon.
"Where's our dinner?" asked the cats. "Where are we supposed to sleep?" asked
the frogs. "We're cold," complained the turtles.

Just then, some fireflies flew overhead. "We're afraid," cried the fish. Now, the rooster really had not made any plans for the trip around the world. He had not remembered to think about food and shelter, so he didn't know how to answer his friends.

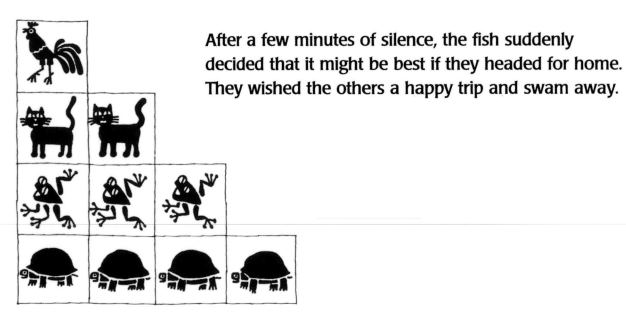

After a few minutes of silence, the fish suddenly
decided that it might be best if they headed for home.
They wished the others a happy trip and swam away.

Then, the turtles began to think about their warm house. They turned and crawled back down the road without so much as a good-bye.

The frogs weren't too happy with the trip anymore, either. First one and then the other and finally the last one jumped away. They were polite enough, though, to wish the rooster a good evening as they disappeared into the night.

The cats then remembered an unfinished meal they had left behind. They kindly wished the rooster a happy journey and they, too, headed for home.

Now the rooster was all alone – and he hadn't seen anything of the world. He thought for a minute and then said to the moon, "To tell you the truth, I am not only hungry and cold, but I'm homesick as well."
The moon did not answer. It, too, disappeared.

The rooster knew what he had to do. He turned around and went back home again.
He enjoyed a good meal of grain and then sat on his very own perch.

After a while he went to sleep and had a wonderful
happy dream – all about a trip around the world!

As a child, Eric Carle claims to have been much more of a philosopher than a mathematician. He recalls his difficulties this way:

"If you told me that there were two apples in a bowl and one was taken away and then asked me how many apples were left I wasn't sure. After all, you can't really take away an apple. You can eat it or make cider out of it or hide it under a basket, but the apple is still an apple and it isn't really gone...

"On the other hand, if you added one apple to a bowl with an apple already in it, there was always the bowl to worry about. Wasn't that a "something" to count in the total?"

Eric Carle wrote Rooster's Off to See the World not only for the child who has these difficulties with numbers as specific symbols, but also for all children who are getting acquainted with numbers.

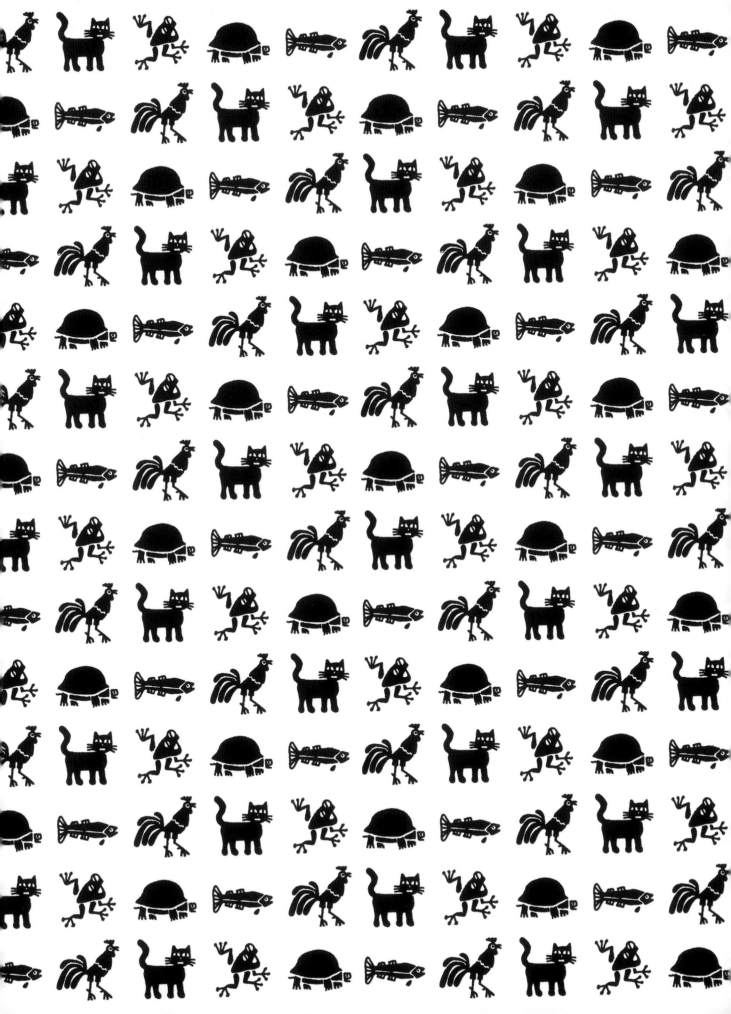